Thomas Warren Field

The School-Mistress in History, Poetry and Romance

Thomas Warren Field

The School-Mistress in History, Poetry and Romance

ISBN/EAN: 9783337348427

Printed in Europe, USA, Canada, Australia, Japan

Cover: Foto ©Andreas Hilbeck / pixelio.de

More available books at **www.hansebooks.com**

THE SCHOOL-MISTRESS

IN

History, Poetry & Romance.

AN ADDRESS

Delivered before the Teachers' Association of the City of Brooklyn,

APRIL 17, 1874.

———•◆•———

Brooklyn:

R. M. WHITING, JR. & CO., PRINTERS, 342 FULTON ST.

—

1874.

ADDRESS.

On this, our first greeting in that natural antagonism of speaker and audience, I have determined that if I have anything of the nature of instruction to give, it shall be inculcated by illustration rather than by dictation. To announce *ex cathedrâ* the duties and privileges of a people, or of a class, is a function bestowed upon only a few; it belongs, doubtless, to the man of God, but seldom to the man of the people.

One reflection which always affects me in assuming the rôle of teacher, is, that society has that somewhat embarrassing habit of requiring the preacher's practice of his own tenets. I am, therefore, timid in propounding educational dogmas, or denouncing long-practised modes as heretical, lest I should be met by that old retort given by the gentlest and divinest Teacher to the Pharisees, beginning with *qui sine peccato.* How needless, too, where the sweet and gentle lives of the good are preaching such divine sermons of unselfish toil, and ceaseless watching over others' good, or those saddest of all lessons, everywhere told on the wayside of life, with the unhappy worshippers of evil, fallen or falling always in our view. Let me then recall from the dim records of the vanishing past the stories of some who have marched before me, or who have been immortalized by imagination and history.

The portfolio of character-pictures I open to you this afternoon is not merely a collection of allegorical designs, but is, when not avowedly drawn from the pages of romance or poetry, a group of portraits of actual and once sentient beings whom I have known.

Few of them are now living, and you may amuse yourselves by fancying that they are recognizable in some you have known, but I assure you that it is scarcely probable (except, perhaps, in clairvoyant perception) that such recognition can be real.

Very early in the world's history, learned ladies assumed the office of instructors; and so potent was their influence that the names and merits of some of them have been ringing through the ages ever since. The daughter of a Greek philosopher rendered her name immortal by the instructions she gave to her father's scholars.

The philosopher indulged himself in such profound reveries on the mysteries of things that this learned lady delivered the addresses of the Academy to throngs of eager pupils. But as she was equally remarkable for her beauty and her learning, the wise old man required her to wear a veil to obscure the charming features of the enchanting lecturess, lest they should distract the attention of his pupils. Who can help regretting that he was not privileged to study in that school? But I think all of our sex would have been constantly praying that the veil should be very thin or altogether be dispensed with.

Through the cloistered aisles of fourteen centuries one name comes like a strain of musical chords from a distant Æolian harp, full of sweetness, but wailing with the sadness of a dirge. It is in the infant years of Christianity, and science herself yet in her cradle, when, in the city which for a thousand years, at the mouth of the Nile, was the queen of commerce, a school which attracted the attention of the learned from all lands was taught by a woman. Her learning and talents commanded the respect of philosophers; her eloquence and wit ravished the admiration of the populace; but her grace of manner and surpassing loveliness of person placed the world at her feet. This learned, accomplished, and beautiful lady was Hypatia, the daughter of an eminent teacher of astronomy, in the Alexandrian or Platonic school, who initiated her into the mysteries of the knowledge then termed science.

The genius of an early writer, who has just left our shores for his native land, has added the charms of fiction to the already romantic fame of Hypatia. You who wish to read her glowing story, which is more history than fiction, even in his book, should seek it in Charles Kingsley's enthralling pages.

The reputation of this lovely instructress for learning had become so established at the period of his death, that she was elected to occupy the chair he had filled with so much celebrity. It was no light honor to be thought worthy of this seat, made eminent by its occupation for one hundred years, with the most eminent professors and instructors of the age. Hamonius, Hierocles, and other famed philosophers of that period, which abounded with learned men, had made it celebrated by their lectures. And now this desk, sacred and imposing, with the memories and fame of the sages who had thence delivered their lessons of wisdom, was filled by a lovely and gentle lady, who inspired her lovers with the devotion of earthly passion, and awed them to humility by the majesty of the divine truths she uttered.

The lectures of Hypatia drew scholars from the most celebrated schools of Greece and Rome, and inspired them with a zeal for learning that made their names immortal.

Synesius, afterwards Bishop of Ptolemais, who was renowned by the writers of that day for the possession of great talents and universal knowledge, became one of her disciples. We have his testimony, joined to that of Socrates, Nicephorus, Gregoras, and many others, to attest the extraordinary learning and genius of Hypatia. " The purity of her morals and the dignified propriety of her conduct commanded reverence and regard from even those who were incompetent to judge of her learning and talents. She was consulted by the magistrates in all cases of difficulty and importance, and her decisions were adopted as the results of judicial acumen and eminent justice."

She frequented the societies of men and lived in the midst of their schools and assemblies with an untarnished reputation; for the lustre of her talents and attainments was softened by the unassuming simplicity of her manners, and the fascinations of her person were chastened by the purity of her life. Her extraordinary attainments, amiable qualities, and bewitching beauty procured her the love and addresses of the most eminent men of the age ; but they besought her for her hand in vain. She had so early fallen deeply in love with science, that her heart would never after admit a rival passion to usurp its place. But although the austerity of her manners could suppress those emotions in her disciples to which her beauty gave birth, yet it could not pre-serve her from the machinations of ambition and revenge. The turbulent and unscrupulous Cyril, Bishop of Alexandria, conceived against her the most malignant hatred on account of her friendship for Orestes, the Roman governor of that city. At a period of great popular frenzy, this ambitious and cruel patriarch caused her to become, by his slanders, the object of hatred to the ignorant and bigoted populace. On returning one day in a sedan from her lecture, she was seized by the merciless mob of Alexandria, stripped naked in the Church of the Cæsars ; her lovely face scarred and gashed by their cruel blows ; her limbs mutilated with scourgings, and at last inhumanly murdered by cutting her to pieces with broken tiles.

As if for ever to hide from human recollection the memory of this execrable deed, her murderers gathered the fragments which had once composed the beautiful body of this accomplished lady, and burned them to ashes in the Cinaron.

The flames which consumed them have illuminated the name and fame of Hypatia the teacher, through

the gloom and shadows of more than fourteen hundred years.

In romance and in satire, there has always been a
mythical character representing the school-mistress
or the master, which has been accepted as the typical representative of their class. How widely this
myth of the scoffing race of scribblers has differed
from the actual instructor, it will be the province of
this essay to discuss.

The carking race of fiction caricaturists, whose
deity is ridicule and whose worship is mockery, have
not scrupled to paint the school-mistress with their
usual cynicism. Let us view the picture drawn by
their pen, dipped in sulphuric acid—the base of which
corrosive agent you all know to be brimstone, an
elementary substance quite appropriate as the me-
dium of their criticism; it is such as they are fond of
depicting her, and the portrait is usually painted
thus.

The typical school-mistress of fiction is a lady of
twenty to fifty years of age, tall, not by any means
ill-looking, who wears convex glasses, which glare
on you like the head-lights of a locomotive, and
thrusts pluperfect participles and isosceles triangles
down your throat on the slightest provocation.

If she ever had a lover, she amazed him to the
borders of epilepsy, or made him a paralytic for life,
by requiring him, on his first visit, as a prelude to
marital intimations, to parse some of the toughest
sentences in *Paradise Lost.*

She is constantly tripping you up for indulging in

vernacular inaccuracies; and, if her admirer ever has the hardihood to offer his heart in exchange for her hand, she replies: "Cannot you contrive, sir, to make your verbs agree with their nominative in number and person?"

She writes treatises on the laws of hygiene, abstains from coffee and hot food, indulges in the mild pleasantry of calling pies poison, and reprimands, with becoming severity, the thoughtless voluptuary who eats candy and drinks lemonade. With all this abstinence, she lives and dies a dyspeptic. The possible enormity of imbibing wine or stronger potations she never permits herself to contemplate; and all the vices, crimes, and frailties of mankind affect her as little as the parallax of Jupiter does the average Patagonian. Should she be accosted at Niagara by an enthusiastic gentleman who incautiously declares the cataract to be the most wonderful object of contemplation in the universe, she would instantly reply: "Sir, you must be profoundly ignorant of the precession of the equinoxes!" Picture, if you can, the dumb astonishment and voiceless depression with which the crushed enthusiast moves away!

Such has the satirist portrayed the mythical teacher, unconscious that beneath the chill demeanor of the pedant, glows a gentle soul that needed only a domestic hearth to kindle with the warmest radiance of wife and mother.

The romancers have done much to envelope the popular conception of the school-mistress with the fallacy which considers her either an ogress or a

sentimentalist. In England, the character is indis-
solubly associated with imbecility and tottering
age ; and the conception has been derived from the
fictions of poets and novelists. From Shenstone to
Dickens, English imaginative works have kept alive
the same antiquated myth ; and no one has done
more to foster and keep alive this legend than the
great novelist just deceased. His rare old school-
dames start up with crutch and switch from the
pages of *David Copperfield* and *Great Expectations ;*
so naturally associated with his wonderful pictures of
boy-life that they do not at all surprise us, but seem
as naturally allied to their adjuncts as do gipsies to a
copse in a quiet dell. Indeed, we expect to greet
one of these venerable school-mistresses, with her
birch and dram, in each of those narratives which
he makes so vivid with the sorrows and trials of the
children of his fancy.

More than a century before, however, the poet
Shenstone had sketched with almost equal strength
of hand his "School-mistress":

> In every village marked with little spire,
> Embowered in trees, and hardly known to fame,
> There dwells, in lowly shed, and mean attire,
> A matron old, whom we school-mistress name ;
> Who boasts unruly brats with birch to tame ;
> They grieven sore, in piteous durance pent,
> Awed by the power of this relentless dame ;
> And ofttimes, on vagaries idly bent,
> For unkempt hair, or task unconned, are sorely shent.
>
> Where sits the dame, disguised in look profound,
> And eyes her fairy throng, and turns her wheel around.
>
> Her cap, far whiter than the driven snow,
> Emblem right meet of decency does yield ;
> Her apron dyed in grain, as blue, I trow,
> As is the harebell that adorns the field ;

And in her hand, for sceptre, she does wield
  Tway birchen sprays; with anxious fear entwined,
With dark distrust, and sad repentance filled;
  And steadfast hate, and sharp affliction joined,
And fury uncontroled, and chastisement unkind.

Right well she knew each temper to descry,
  To thwart the proud, and the submiss to raise;
Some with vile copper prise exalt on high,
  And some entice with pittance small of praise;
And other some with baleful sprig she 'frays:
  Even absent, she the reins of power doth hold,
While with quaint arts the giddy crowd she sways;
  Forewarned, if little bird their pranks behold,
'Twill whisper in her ear, and all the scene unfold.

Lo! now with state she utters her command;
  Eftsoons the urchins to their task repair,
Their books of stature small they take in hand,
  Which with pellucid horn secured are,
To save from finger wet the letters fair:
  The work so gay, that on their back is seen,
St. George's high achievements does declare;
  On which thilk wight that has y-gazing been,
Kens the forthcoming rod—unpleasing sight, I ween.

Out of the pages of romance have sprung also
some of the most nobly human characters, which re-
present the instructress as woman in her best estate,
whom satire has not deformed, and caricature un-
sexed. Such will you find in the portrait which
Charlotte Brontë has drawn of her own right
womanly self in *Jane Eyre* and *Villette;* women
whom I am grateful that it has been my fortune to
know living, breathing examples of.

What fine, noble creatures of fancy and nature
in partnership they were, making the world glad and
good wherever they went! Not angels altogether,
though, for the sharpness of resentfulness is an absolute need in woman's most exalted character. The
grape-sugar which gives the golden wine of Tokay
its bouquet and flavor is not sweet; it is represented in

the chemist's laboratory by a compound of cane-sugar and—and—can I say it?—sulphuric acid.

Villette is a poetess in her sensibilities, a Sister of Charity in her devotion to her pupils, but a woman in her social resentments. How she does detest, with a poet's refinement, a nun's charity and a woman's antipathy, the cautious, composed, and absorbingly selfish Madame Beck, principal of the school! And when the cat-like movements of this most excellent, but most suspicious lady, reveal her presence only by her shadow, how involuntarily our teacher shudders, as though she had seen the ghost which nightly frightens her superstitious pupils. But Madame Beck is herself a fine conception of the teacher in whom the woman has been mostly absorbed. Conscientious, sly, suspicious, generous, and religious in her way, she is a teacher to be prized, if not a woman to be loved.

The portrait painted by the master-limner Dickens, is of a lineal descendant of Shenstone's original, and perhaps a faithful counterfeit of one he had known forty years before.

Listen to his inimitable description of Pip's first school :

"The educational scheme, or course, established by Mr. Wopsley's great-aunt, may be resolved into the following synopsis :

"The pupils ate apples, and put straws down one another's backs, until Mr. Wopsley's great-aunt collected her energies, and made an indiscriminate totter at them with a birch rod. After receiving the charge with every form of derision, the pupils formed in line, and buzzingly passed a ragged book from hand to hand. The book had an alphabet in it, some figures and tables, and a little spelling; that is to say—it had once.

"As soon as the volume began to circulate, Mr. Wopsley's great-aunt fell into a state of coma, arising either from sleep or a rheumatic paroxysm. The pupils then entered among themselves upon a competitive examination on the subject of boots, with the view of ascertaining who could tread the hardest upon whose toes. This part of the course was usually lightened by several single combats between them and Biddy, the maid-of-all-work of Mr. Wopsley, and Mr. Wopsley's great-aunt's assistant. When the fights were over, Biddy gave out the number of a page, then we all read aloud what we could, or rather what we couldn't, in a frightful chorus; Biddy leading with a high, shrill, monotonous voice, and none of us having the least notion of, or reverence for, what we were reading. When this horrible din had lasted a certain time, it mechanically awoke Mr. Wopsley's great-aunt, who staggered at a boy fortuitously, and pulled his ears. This was understood to terminate the course for the evening, and we emerged into the air with the shrieks of intellectual victory."

Having once opened the pages of this necromancer, it is impossible to resist their magic influence. As they have charmed me to acquiescence, so must you listen, though never so reluctant, to one or two more excerpts from them. It is something worthy of remark that most of the vulgar heroes and heroines of Dickens's creation have the most sublime respect for the graces of education.

Joe Gargery announces his serious convictions regarding them with a sagacity and precision which would do honor to some learned theorists of our days :

"Well, Pip," said Joe, "be it so or be it son't, you must be a common scholar, afore you can be a on-common one, I should hope? The king upon his throne, with his crown upon his 'ed, can't sit and write his h'acts of parliament in print, without having begun when he were an unpromoted prince with the halphabet. Ah," added he, with a shake of the head that was full of meaning, "and begun with A, too, and worked his way to Zed, and I know what that is to do—though I can't ezactly say I've hever done it."

The theorists we have referred to, who are so fond of speculation on the influences which go to affect the expanding of the juvenile intellect, are often vastly further astray than poor Joe. They remind me of the sapient Dogberry, whose enunciations upon learning rival theirs in profundity.

I find it quite impossible to resist the temptation of presenting to you that exquisite satire upon these wiseacres which Pip's further experience in learning furnishes. That dastardly humbug, Pumblechook, must have his turn at the educational mill ; or, rather, the inquisitorial rack.

Pip is at breakfast, as it is served in Pumblechook's kitchen, when the torture begins. "I considered (says Pip) Mr. Pumblechook wretched company, for his conversation consisted of nothing but arithmetic. On my politely bidding him good-morning, he said pompously: 'Seven times nine, boy?' Now, how should I be able to answer, dogged in that way, in a strange place, on an empty stomach? I was very hungry; but before I had swallowed a morsel, he began a running sum that lasted all through break-fast. 'Seven,' 'and four,' and 'eight and six?' 'and two and ten?' and so on. And after each figure was disposed of, it was as much as I could do to get a bite or a sup before the next came; while he sat at his ease, guessing nothing, and eating bacon and hot roll in—if I may be allowed the expression—a gorging and gormandizing man-ner."

So strongly impressed was Mr. Pumblechook with the tranquillizing, not to say subduing, effect of numbers upon youthful depravity, that three hours later, after accompanying Pip to Miss Habi-sham's house, he had, as Pip hoped, finally departed, when he reopened the gate, thrust forward his fish-head to propound with great impressiveness the problem—"And fourteen?"

But the wise theorists, on modes and plans of edu-cation, had an origin far earlier than Dickens's days. Shakespeare himself must have had experience of their impertinent interference in his boyhood, for even the sapient Dogberry must have his specula-tions upon learning and tuition. In the third scene of the third act of "Much Ado about Nothing," he addresses thus his brother constable: "Come hither, neighbor Seacole; God hath blessed thee with a good name. To be a well-favored man is the gift of fortune. But to write and to read comes by nature." And afterwards he adds: "Well, for your favor, sir; why, give God thanks. But for your reading and writing, let that appear when there is need of such vanity."

Midway between the school-mistress of fiction and the practical everyday lady with whom we are some--what familiar, dwells a character not commonly found in our work-a-day world, nor wholly unknown to the poet and novelist.

The philosophical schoolmam dwells in a practical world; the mythical teacher only in the brain of the malignant caricaturist. The two representations, the imaginative and the real, are widely diverse in their motive, and yet similar in their peculiarities; they are like in their very unlikeness. The feminine philosopher views everything from the stand-point of a syllogism—thus: "Sir, either a thing is, or it is not. If it is not, then it cannot be a thing; for thing implies existence, and the not being is no thing or nothing. If it is, then it is indisputable; for to discuss it you admit that it has existence precisely as it is—you admit everything, therefore you have nothing to discuss." By the time this syllogistic whirlpool has ceased, the bewildered listener is in a state of moderate catalepsy. Thus reasoning with infinite no-reason, she will prove that nothing is equal to everything. She is learned in Wheatley and Stewart and Sir William Hamilton; has read Comte and Lewes and Herbert Spencer; has the skilfully prepared baits of argument always ready to set alluringly the logical trap, which infallibly snaps your fingers off if you once touch the tempting morsel. Critical to the last degree of refinement, she permits you to become involved in a conversational

labyrinth by the enticement of some Jack-'o-lantern
glimmer of statement ; and then snap go the jaws of
the argumentative trap, and she complacently tri-
umphs over your bewilderment. In school she is
exact and rigid in the performance of her duties, and
visits with eminent severity the delinquencies of her
pupils. Merciless to herself, in compelling her very
physical infirmities to yield to her mental vigor
with relentless self-control; she looks upon the laxity
of others with a sort of horror. Her pupils usually
excel in scholarship and are models of propriety,
but they go out into the world to learn somewhat
late, that it is filled with a very commonplace and
lax humanity. Solecisms of language are offences
which her pupils would rather commit suicide than
incur her scornful indignation for perpetrating. Her
slight tendency to cynicism is evidenced by frequent
quotations from Carlyle, but her passion for the mild
mysticism of Emerson transcends that of a romantic
school-girl for a dime novel.

She recites with infinite satisfaction the erudite
and slightly mystic Brahma:

> If the red slayer think he slays,
>   Or if the slain think he is slain,
> They know not well the subtle ways
>   I keep and pass and turn again.
>
> They reckon ill who leave me out ;
>   When me they fly, I am the wings ;
> I am the doubter and the doubt,
>   And I the hymn the Brahmin sings.
>
> The strong gods pine for my abode,
>   And pine in vain the sacred Seven ;
> But thou, meek lover of the good,
>   Find me, and turn thy back on heaven.

Her longings for the infinite are always tinged with the indefinite. They are so profound in their aspirations as to be usually far deeper than the soundings of her reason; and she has always the most maidenly unconsciousness that they would be perfectly satisfied with a loving husband and a modest home.

Her teaching is eminently practical, severe in its conformity to literalness, but honest and thorough. There is no slipshod, shuffling work; no neglected corners in the housewifery of her tuition.

Nor is her instruction confined to the strict outline and detail of study; for her hatred of sham and delusion impels her to strip the tinsel rags from off the strutting pageants so common on the stage of life. The illusory scenes in its drama, which so beguile school-girls, she especially delights in exposing. The paltry shifts, the golden crowns made of scrap-tin, the splendid castles, hanging gardens, lengthening vistas of patriarchal oaks, and boundless parks, she glories in showing to be only the reverse of rotting canvas, cobwebs, dirt, and tumble-down carpentry, which would shame a country blacksmith-shop. In this her practical scepticism has almost priceless utility. The romantic school-girl just lapsing into love-sickness, is well-nigh cured by one of her teacher's powerful tonics.

The glamour of fiction has often, with the power of Oberon's spell, made the inamoratas of young girls seem to be princes, or at the least counts in disguise—but one mocking phrase of our female Mentor destroys the illusion and reveals them to be only barber's apprentices. The heroes they were ready to adore with all a woman's devotion and a girl's folly, prove under the relentless scrutiny of our philosopher in crinoline, to be car-drivers.

For poetry and romance she entertains the most sovereign contempt, and looks upon indulgence in their fictitious joys and woes as intellectual suicide. She has heard of Dickens and Thackeray, but should some incautious friend refer to *Clive New-come* or *Pickwick*, he is lost. She turns with a severity in her countenance that convinces him, before she speaks, of the frightful turpitude of his offence : " Sir, I have read something of history attentively, but I never before heard of the characters you have named. I must therefore conclude that you obtained your information regarding them from fiction ; they, consequently, never had an existence, and cannot be quoted as authorities."

Let no one cherish the unjust reflection that, amid those rhapsodies, our philosopher schoolmam has not the most loyal devotion to the subjects of her duty. Whimsical, erratic, transcendental she may be, but true woman, underneath all, in her almost chivalrous loyalty to her profession. She resents, with fervid indignation, the lightest scoffing at her vocation, and momentarily forgets the ponder-ous rule she has adopted in her scheme of feminine philosophy. This formula is usually announced at the commencement of a discussion—thus: " Sir, let us investigate this important subject with dispassion-ate ratiocination." All other subjects than that of her occupation she finds little difficulty in treating with this amiable philosophy ; to her they have but slight personal interest, for, be it literature, theology,

or metaphysics, she thinks of it only in the concrete
—the æsthetic. No matter what she proves, it is that
undying motive-power of her sex which incites her
—the love of conquest. But her face flushes with
honest wrath when the duties and labors of her
vocation are depreciated, and nature asserts itself
over factitious philosophy. The ponderous style of
her arguing mood vanishes, and the clear, terse language of her vernacular comes bursting from her
lips, in tones somewhat shrill and vehement.

She looks with chill severity through the convex
lens which make her gaze seem still more icy, upon
the whining beggar, and refuses, in tones so quiet,
yet so firm, that the mendicant declines to add his
usual sickly plaint of thirteen children and no bread.
But in the dusk of evening, clothed in her modest
school-hat, her plainest shawl, and an abundant
mantle of charity, she glides out to the sad home of
a sick scholar, where lean poverty hides itself
under the threadbare cloak of respectability.

Her own scanty savings are drawn liberally upon
for his comfort, and her classic mask of philosophy
drops to reveal the surpassing loveliness of one of
God's ministering angels.

But in the solitary room of the chill boarding-
house, to which her narrow income has condemned
her, other and warmer fancies will introduce themselves. She may, like Elizabeth Barrett Browning,

> " Sit still
> On winter nights by lonely fires, and hope,
> To hear the nations praising her far off."

But she is more likely to be sitting with dull fire,

and aching with sick heart, amid all her philosophy, for the placid comfort of something dependent and loving. All that elaborate misery she is so fond of depicting in her philosophizing moods as *the teasing vexations of domestic infelicity* has disappeared in the gloom of her chamber, and she is once more the unaffected scholar, the gentle, kindly teacher, all human and all woman. We will not darken our picture by imagining her—perhaps desperate in her loneliness—to be deluded by the specious or mercenary affection of some traitor lover, while in a midsummer-night's dream

> "She, poor lady, dotes,
> Devoutly dotes, dotes in idolatry,
> Upon this spotted and inconstant man."

Let us rather believe that her cold philosophy melts away in the generous sunlight of a happy home, and that in her reveries the sweet jangle of far-off wedding-bells are only anticipations of an assured reality.

But what of the real everyday school-teacher—one of the twenty-five thousand of the State of New York —our flesh-and-blood girl representative of that army of more than two hundred thousand of her sex which, in these United States, is arrayed against ignorance and vice? If the occasional eccentricities of her profession are worth picturing by every presumptuous hand, she is a subject for the master's pencil and palette. Perhaps it is the ruddy-cheeked, full-chested farmer's daughter whose studies have filled the intellectual measure of a rural academy, and who, adown some winding, high-banked country road is tripping on a spring morning, to the little red school-house, that looks like a sentry-box perched on a bank to guard a neighboring wood. And so it is, thank God, a guard-house on the frontier line of an enemy's territory, and our little woman stands guard right soldierly against a most insidious and deadly foe. She does not look like it, brightly stepping down that country lane, over which, but for the new dignity of school-mistress, she would take an honest race with the urchins who are clambering and shouting by her side. In her full healthfulness and glee, inspired by the rich blood of the strong farmer-race from which she sprang, she heartily wishes it was the proper thing for her to untie that jaunty summer-hat, and, with it trailing by the strings, go chasing the apple-cheeked boys and girls across the neighboring meadow.

How came she here, armed with her meed of learning, enlisted in this war on ignorance ? Somewhere back in her brief history an electric spark from the great galvanic-battery of knowledge awakened her dormant mind to a new life. Thought added to thought built up a soul in that healthy body, untenanted hitherto, or, if so, totally unconscious of its occupant. As the world which book telescopes opened to her vision expanded, she became conscious that more strong-armed brothers were growing up around her than the scant farm would find sustenance for. One of these embryo agriculturists became infected with his sister's love of books, and him she determined to send to that Mecca of the devotees of learning—the college. But the resources of the narrow, hard-tilled acres forbade the expenditure of even the meagre sum needed for that purpose, in this land of colleges. So she applied for and received the appointment of teacher in that red sentry-box on the border of the wood, whither she is going on this spring morning, wishing she could swing her hat by its fluttering ribbons and chase away across the adjoining meadow. The windows of this temple of learning, or rather of this modest porch to the temple, open on one side directly upon the narrow road, and on the other upon a field, now a meadow, but later in the season a pasture, where a lowing herd of cattle range, sheltering themselves during the hot mid-day in the shade of the school-house. Sometimes Deacon Prayall's great bull comes bellowing defiantly under the open windows with a fit of belligerency, excited by the low of a distant rival, or, more probably, exasperated by some wicked urchin who has slyly shook his red bandanna handkerchief out of the window. Our healthful school-mistress does not care for a romp on that meadow just now. And what do you think is the magnificent sum-total of her remuneration for this service of standing guard, and sometimes actually skirmishing against the enemy with a switch from the conveniently neighboring wood ? Why, less than one hundred dollars of legal currency for a year's service, or rather for the six months to which her educational duties are confined by the economy of her patrons. In a year or two her success is so marked that some prowling superintendent, dull-eyed and fritter-brained as he may be, discovers her ability, and goes gossiping about, saying in the neighboring town, "Smart girl that of Farmer

Broadback's, up in District Twenty. She'll beat your long-legged college chap you've got over in the Union School." And so our ruddy country school-mam is translated to a two-story school-house, painted a dazzling white, instead of the sanguinary litharge of that guard-house by the wood.

The collegian is from this time a better-dressed man, and on commencement day a demure but glad-looking young woman sits in front of him as he orates on the forum. How proudly and lovingly she looks at him, this clergyman in the milk, and wonders if she will live to bring father and mother some day to hear John preach. I don't know whether our little mistress continued in the Union School until the bright eyes grew dim enough for spectacles, went on a mission to China, or leaned tenderly en the arm of some tall, broad-chested fellow, down the thorough-fare of life. If the last, I warrant the small round arm was clasped tightly between that great biceps and the broad chest. Accursed, thrice accursed of God and men and angels, be the wretch who shall loosen with insidious wiles that clasp, or darken their hearth-stone with the baleful shadow of a hateful presence !

Perhaps in the long vacation she ekes out her in-come by service, which in the towns would be thought degrading and menial, but in the wholesome regions of New Hampshire and Vermont is not deemed servile. During my summer tour through the extensive area of territory occupied by the range of the White Mountains, I was much interested by the peculiar character of the ladies and gentlemen who officiated as waiters at the hotels. It is by no means a rhetorical stretch of veracity to say, that in all the graces of erudition, in classical and other scholastic attainments, they were vastly the superiors of the richly-dressed guests who sat at the tables attended by them. Several hundreds of the students of Amherst and Dartmouth Colleges and of the seminaries and academies of New England (and teachers of rural districts), found not only remunerative employment, but a generous accession of health and vitality in their honorable service in the mountains. Nor were they without honest respect and honorable consideration by even the haughty devotees of fashion. The most supercilious of that long train had a more courteous and gentle air, in the presence of these educated and refined young men and women, who honored them by their own courteous attendance. A graduate of Harvard University officiated as dining-room usher at one hotel; and a graduate of Amherst who was studying for the bar was his assistant. Not a few of the female waiters were school teachers, thus profitably employing and enjoying their vacation.

Shall we look upon a darker picture, before which hangs a veil obscuring scenes that sorrow has already sufficiently darkened? In the broad world of life there lies many a deep valley which the slant sun-rays of joy never brighten. Our gentle mistress sometimes descends sorrowfully, tearfully, down its rugged sides [for the husband she has chosen is not always just or gentle], and thereafter she dwells in its dreary shadow, until lifted by God's angels into the cloudless sunshine of his presence. There is many a pretty Titania madly in love with a transformed Bottom, whose ass's ears are not adorned with eglan-tine; whose features are akin to the self-drawn picture of Mirabeau: "A tiger's face pitted with the small-pox." But Titania sees only with crazed eyes, and her lunatic affection has clothed him with the beauty of Adonis. His soul may be a fit companion for its brutal lodgment, dwelling for ever in hateful contriv-ings against the peace and love he hates and scorns, yet her sick fancy has made it radiant with the halo of a seraph.

He may come to her feculent with the impurity of infamy, or reeking with the fumes of his mid-night orgies, and her dead senses convey no alarm to her doting heart.

He carries desolation and sorrow wherever he goes. His foot-fall on the doorstep is a knell to his friend's household; his words, poison; his presence, death. And yet, supported by that mysterious sleep-walking instinct which perceives nothing by the senses, she lives and loves through all. Vulgar in his manners —brutal in his instincts—foul in his morals—traitor in his friendship—and false in his love, he is the type and climax of heroism and manhood to her per-verted sense. And so, till he abandons her a wreck floating out upon that ocean which is always ebbing, farther and farther into the shadow, and beyond which is no port, no continent or island, which human eye has ever seen.

Over this picture let the curtain fall. The mists and clouds which darken it can never shut it from our mental vision, but a brighter, because a holier one, will substitute its radiant scenes.

Our gentle world of modest instructors is not without its saints ; even if poor in the sterner virtue of martyrs. The cloisters do not contain all who have devoted themselves to perpetual self-abnegation, chastity, and good works.

One such I knew—yes, know—though long since not of this world. Her school children had been noted for the sweetness and pathos of their singing. When the full chorus of their well-trained voices carolled joyously, like a flock of uncaged birds, or melted away in some plaintive note that told of human grief and angelic pity, or rose in swelling strains of exultation over the sorrows of earth, the passers in the neighboring street paused, listening to the sweet rapture-tones, until the unwilling tears forced themselves from eyes long dried in the fierce heat of greed and strife of commerce or ambition.

There were those who thought they heard the voices of their own beloved children, that died long years ago, heard as echoes from the far-off heaven; but some, whose thoughts ever after dwelt upon the ravishing sweetness of a broken strain which reached them, they knew not from whence, always half-believed they had heard the singing of the holy children, that stand in white robes before the divine Teacher, whose lessons were given on the slopes of Olivet.

And thenceforth these went about with a low refrain of infant music lingering in their ears, and perhaps tuning their souls to a better life.

Did the gentle songs she had taught her sweet-voiced pupils make her envious of that holy choir, chanting far beyond the sea of Galilee?

Day by day she faded, and long before the dark angel's wings waved over her pallid face, she, too, heard the voices of an infinite host of children singing, and in her sick fancy she knew the tones of some whom she had taught; and so, listening raptured, her soul floated out beyond the cloud and shadow which hides that choir from us.

But not alone in those modest structures on green lanes, or bordered by woods and meadows, are to be found the self-denial, patience, and talent which are devoted to dispelling the darkness of ignorance.

Our rural teacher has sisters, who, eager to know more of that bustling world which every summer sends its idlers and convalescents strolling by her school-door; stray off to the great cities, and there find that their firm muscles and healthy brains fit them to cope with their metropolitan cousins. They find, too, that self-devotion and zeal are not confined to those of rural birth, but that the teeming city breeds its hundreds of noble-hearted women who bravely maintain the struggle of knowledge against ignorance. In a metropolitan city there is a district where poverty is queen, and sways her sceptre over thousands of pallid subjects at whose cabin doors sits lean Hunger, and within Disease an unbidden guest, hollow-eyed and spectral, lingers always. In this noisome and pestilential territory the teeming multitudes of little humanities had found that priceless blessing, a wise and faithful teacher—a woman of more than ordinary culture, possessed of qualities of mind and graces of person, that made her a welcome guest and an envied friend. She assumed the guardianship of this host of little savages when a great public school was founded in the midst of their squalid habitations. In their persons, scarcely concealed by unseemly rags, and in their faces, hardly recognizable, from day to day, by new accretions of dirt and smudge, the teacher, by sheer force of conscience, compelled her sensibilities to perceive nothing but sacred humanity. In their feeble intellects, she saw only torpidity; and in their perverted morals, nothing but ignorance.

Beneath the grime and gloom she perceived in each squalid little form a sleeping soul—a chrysalis which could be wakened into immortal beauty. And so, in her hearty, simple faith she could see how ignorance and vice were to be charmed away from poverty and sorrow; by the gentle influences of kindness and education. Oh! holy and beautiful charity; though gracious and winning in all, how resplendent in supernal loveliness art thou in womanhood.

I cannot here recite the incidents of that long battle with Ignorance and his pallid sister Vice. Day after day, and week after week, she struggled with depraved habits, with reckless and wanton defiance, and resentment of her instructions, yet day after day she was gaining a more defensible lodgment in this stronghold of misery.

Aided by a determined will, a strong, full-pulsing heart, and woman's trustfulness, she wrought at last a wondrous change, and when another brave woman, with equal intelligence and heartfulness, devoted herself to the same task, in another part of this debatable land, where "night and morning were at meeting," the work was already half-accomplished. The lady who had become so powerful an auxiliary saw that complete victory could only be obtained by storming the enemy's stronghold, and conquering the vicious domestic habits. So, enforced by her corps of gentle yet brave assistants, she commenced a new crusade.

The dirtiest of the little barbarians were accordingly subjected to a system of detergent scouring, which often resulted in producing a stranger face beneath the mask of grime, who ran the risk of rejection from his astonished parents. Their ragged garments, patched and mended into decency, not unfrequently added to the illusion.

Those reformed street gipsies were thus deputed as missionaries of cleanliness to their own homes, and not unfrequently were followed by these undaunted ladies, who enforced the lesson their labors suggested.

These gracious toils were not bestowed in vain, and if the irrefutable testimony of facts regarding their success can yield them any gratification, they ought to reap ·abundant pleasure from its contemplation. Orderly, neat, and intelligent pupils now throng from homes of exceeding penury and destitution, yet wholesome in their cleanliness. Wherever generous self-denial and modest but o'ercoming labor for others' good are appreciated, let these ladies' services for humanity and learning be honored and esteemed. Of one such sang our own Longfellow:

> She dwells by great Kenhawa's side,
> In valleys green and cool,

And all her hope and all her pride
Are in her village school.

Her soul, like the transparent air
That robes the hills above,
Though not of earth, encircles there
All things with arms of love.

And thus she walks amid her girls,
With praise and mild rebukes ;
Subduing e'en rude village churls,
By her angelic looks.

As I approach the threshold of school-houses where such labors have been performed (and there are more than one in this city), I am sensible of an o'ercoming tenderness that befits more properly another sex. But when I look along the ranks of upturned faces, youthful in physiognomical proportions, but aged with premature care and privation, while behind the senile mask fitful gleams of childish laughter are struggling, it is then I find the tears lie near the surface and hard to be repressed.

But we must not think of our everyday schoolmistress, as all instructress and little of woman.

The drilling in hard facts has not squeezed out the warm blood of gentleness from her veins and left her nothing but ossified channels of circulation, without a generous pulse in them to beat in sympathy with a child's sorrows. The dreadful formulas which harrow the souls of so many little urchins under the Gradgrind system of instruction, arouse a tender pity in her for the puzzled brains and aching hearts appalled at the formidable tasks before them.

You remember that exquisite satire of Dickens on an iron course of study, which that eminent teacher,

Mr. McChoakumchild, declared Cissy Jupe had per-
versely failed to get any benefit from. He reported
to the committee "that she had a very dense head
for figures; that, once possessed with a general idea
of the globe, she took the smallest conceivable interest in its exact measurements; that she was ex-
tremely slow in the acquisition of dates, unless some
pitiful incident happened to be connected therewith;
that she would burst into tears on being required (by
the mental process—now called intellectual arithmetic)
immediately to name the cost of two hundred and
forty-seven muslin night-caps at fourteen pence half-
penny each; that after an eight weeks' course in
the elements of political economy, she had only yes-
terday replied to the question, "What is the first
principle of the science of political economy?" with
the absurd answer, "To do to others as I would that
they should do to me."

The local committee of the day were horrified at
this monstrous proposition of the duties of govern-
ments, and Mr. Gradgrind observed, shaking his
head: "That all this was very bad, that it showed
the necessity of infinite grinding at the mill of knowledge as per system (course of study), schedule, blue-
book, report, and tabular statements A to Z; and
that Jupe must be kept to it. So Cissy Jupe was
kept to it, and became very low-spirited, but *no*
wiser."

Our flesh-and-blood school-mistress has little in
sympathy with Mr. Choakumchild and his iron system, and yet her voice gets somewhat shrill, and her
intonations border on the vehement, when her instructions are wantonly violated, or she has dealings

in the after-school hours with the reprobate or indo-
lent. I am not fond of contemplating her at anything but her best, and yet I am not sorry that the
saccharine constitution of her disposition, is gently
acidulated, by the citric acid of high spirit and some
temper.

The everyday life which seems so commonplace
and tame, when passed within the walls of the school-
room is not without its evidences of heroism. An occupation assumed at first with the baldest purposes of
thrift, becomes clothed in after-years with something
almost sacred, as the power for good or ill slowly
but unceasingly develops its dread extent to the educated sense. At first, it seems a feeble scope for the
employment of the full intellect of man or woman
aspiring perhaps to literary or social distinction, and
impatient of the paltry details and petty restraints of
school life ; perhaps always urged on in study or in-
vestigation by that indefinable longing with which the
curse of Eve's transgression has infected the acquisition of learning. But as the avenues to influence
over the dawning intellects in her charge open wider
and lengthen, the importance of securing their occupation before ignorance has closed, or superstition
narrowed them ;—her vocation is elevated in her ap-
preciation. It is indeed a task, if you consider it
rightfully, full of awe, and not to be lightly entered
upon. They are not few in number in whose perception this sentiment has grown to apprehension—
grown until a sense of awful responsibility oppresses
their consciences with a weight they can neither less-
en nor escape. The incompleteness of all modes of

tuition becomes painfully apparent, and the imperfection of much of its machinery saddens and disheartens them. The waste of a human life seems such a dreadful loss; and they arraign themselves sometimes with it as the result of their negligence for an hour. During the period of my more intimate and official relations with the teachers of Brooklyn, nothing has affected me more deeply, than the prevalence of this constantly increasing responsibility. The peculiarities of its exhibition and the incidents associated with it, would form a curious chapter in the history of education. More than once I have been requested by ladies with such especial and almost tearful earnestness, to anticipate the period of examination of their classes, that the curiosity which my sex possesses in common with theirs, impelled me to seek the reason for such vehement pertinacity. It was not, however, until the period of an impending event became imminent, that their maidenly reserve yielded to their apprehensions, and they informed me that unless my examination of their classes could take place immediately, their wedding-day must be postponed. For even with that one event close approaching, which crowns with its golden coronet a maiden's life, the intense subjection of their souls to the high duty they had assumed, forbade its abandonment without official approval of their services, as a sort of treason.

Need I say that such delicate consciousness of duty, seemed to bestow additional loveliness on forms and features already sufficiently endowed with grace and beauty.

May the melody of their wedding-bells fill long

and happy lives with their blessed music, and be heard dying away in the distance like an echo, when that saddest peal of all is tolling!

But keen susceptibility to the exacting duties of your profession is not confined to those who succeed in it.

Application was once made to me by a lady, whose scholarship and ability abundantly fitted her for the task, for appointment to a vacancy in a primary department. The lady, I was confident by personal knowledge, possessed every quality which could assure me of her ultimate success, and I was happy in being able at once to comply with her request. The position was not by any means commensurate in grade, with the high qualities of which she was in possession, and the compensation was correspondingly meagre. I was, however, fully aware that the small remuneration was of no light importance; nay, was of almost absolute necessity to her. My surprise, therefore, was extreme, when, before the lapse of a month, she called upon me to tender her resignation, saying with quiet, yet firm dignity, that she had discovered that the tuition of a class of that grade was a task she was not fitted for; and the sense of her failure to accomplish all which it had the right to demand, compelled her to resign.

Her eminent capabilities and accomplishments found a channel for their utility; her self-abnegation and honesty brought a just reward; for her genius not long after opened a path to reach a height of fame which is the fortune of but few of her sex.

The authoress of many esteemed books, and the

translator and editress of meritorious works from the French, she now presides over a noble journal of such popularity and profit that her remuneration is not exceeded by that of any editor in this country.

Nor are instances of heroism confined to in-structors; for as you become more intimately acquainted with the fortunes and needs of your pupils, you will discover qualities of mind, and instances of heroic self-denial, which will elicit your interest and excite your admiration. You will see the evidences of bitter, stinging poverty, struggling with eager sensibility, at once to hide its necessities and to provide for the education of loved ones, as a means of admission to respectability and usefulness. I can never withhold the tribute of my deep respect, for hundreds of such heroes and heroines of the domestic field of honor. One that always affects my sensibility, near to the borders of manly self-control, I cannot resist the temptation to relate to you. In a school of this city, where the hard necessities of poverty, for ever warring with an insatiate appetite for learning, finds many of its youthful victims, one family especially afford a noble example of the conquest of intellectual over physical necessities.

It consists of seven gentle, well-trained children, supported by the labor of a father whose highest wages, never exceed the enviable remuneration of two dollars per day. Every session of the school finds all of these devotees of learning in attendance, orderly in manners, neat in dress, and scholarly in their duties. The home from which they come, humble to the last degree of penury, seems to me enshrined in a halo of sanctity, which makes it grander than a cathedral.

Forty years have come and gone since an instructress of girls made a city on the Hudson celebrated for the excellence of her school, almost as widely as it has since been for its gigantic works in iron. A woman whose intellectuality would have distinguished her in literature; whose strong, firm sense would have conquered success in great commercial enterprise; whose logical and healthy brain would have given her eminence at the bar; and whose eloquence and piety assured her of distinction in the pulpit, established here an institution of learning which made her influence felt for three generations. Although the style and title of her school had no more pretentious claim than "Young Ladies' Seminary," yet she was effectually the president of a college, as potent in its influence on the intellects and culture of the time, as any of the more imposing universities. The very atmosphere of her school was vitalized by intellectual ozone, that stimulated the minds of her pupils to the highest exertion. Such elasticity and inspiration did they draw from it, that even those mental organisms which seemed feeble or dormant, were vivified by it to a high intellectuality, and grew strong under her training. All that was possible in the scope and range of thought of her pupils she evolved; and there went out from her seminary, during the thirty years she ruled over it, many hundreds of cultivated and scholarly young women, whose influence in disseminating refinement and stimulating the acquisition of learning, was felt for half a century at the bar, in the halls of legislation, in the sacred desk, the conduct of public journals, in literature, in art and commerce.

Her vigorous mentality and scrupulous industry impelled all minds along the channel of her intellect, and activity was constantly induced by such words as those of the wise Hebrew king:

" Whatsoever thy hand findeth to do, do with·thy might; for there is no work, nor device, nor knowledge, nor wisdom, in the grave whither thou goest."

" Do you not know;"—we may suppose she thus enforces the injunction ;—"that to some young humanity here each day's tuition may be the last, as it is possible each may be yours." .

" And do you remember what Empedocles says in his quaint old denunciation of the Agrigentines, whose city was filled with massive and gorgeous buildings, while its citizens were sunk in luxury and debauchery :—That they abandoned themselves to voluptuousness as if every day was to be their last; and they built as if they were never to die ?—Now, reflect that the sensuous old theology of the Greeks taught them to enjoy the present to its highest, because the future was uncertain—the purer philosophy of the Christian impels him to make the future certain by using well the present."

Thus this wise instructress taught the troops of laughing, pleasure-loving girls which thronged her school, to become not only well-bred and learned women, but intelligent, sagacious, true, and loving wives and mothers ; from whom sprang a race of sons and daughters, with a reverence for learning, a love of goodness, and an honest hatred of the false and unjust, which has not yet, thank heaven! died out in their descendants.

If there was any one train of excellence which was

pre-eminent in this noble teacher, it was her detesta-
tion of shams, and wherever a fallacy or an affec-
tation showed its hateful presence, her resistless scorn
for ever deprived it of the power to deceive.

Eminent in learning and its diffusion, Mrs. Willard
was equally distinguished in literature and science.
As an authoress, her works gave her fame only less
extended than her tuition, and her labors in the cause
of humanity would have been deemed great had she
not already such celebrity as an instructress.

When, full of days and honors, this excellent lady—
learned, wise, and discreet—was slowly yielding her
soul to immortality, there was many a proud and
noble matron, many a beautiful and gentle woman,
adown whose cheeks stole the tears of grief and affection—and so, loving and beloved, she went to her
rest.

Thirty years ago, I commenced my association with
education as an instructor in the Island City—foster-
mother of our own, and twenty years are almost
closing their cycle of a score, since I was selected to
direct its interests in the Board of Education.

Along this extended plane of life, whose farther
extreme is vanishing into the dim obscure of a past
eternity, my retrospective view perceives a thousand
forms of those youthful instructors, who thronged
each year with hopefulness and anticipation, whom
it was my good fortune to foster or induct into
their coveted places as teachers.   In that period more
than three thousand young girls have risen from the
rank of pupils to the commissions of instructors;
and thirty-six thousand have finished the higher

course of studies, and perhaps as wives and mothers, are now inspiring their offspring with lessons, learned from tongues which are for ever silent in this world.

I look down the long vista of faces, back-turned to me from the farther land, and I see a thousand saddened, and a thousand glad. Some, refined by sorrow, seemed to lose even here the grossness of mortality, and to acquire the spiritual essence long before their souls were freed from its earth-born encumbrance. And some, O relentless, inseparable twins of Destiny, Shame, and Sorrow ! how remorselessly ye pursued the poor fugitive souls to their death—not death, indeed, either, though they died long ago to the better life—the sweet maidens whom I knew with breath daintier than summer violets, and thoughts pure as an infant's dreams.

Drop the curtain over these pictures of hope and sorrow. The shadows are gathering faster and faster, and are enclosing from mortal vision the forms of those we loved and mourn. And the one thought which stretches out its infinite longings towards them for ever retreating into the shadow, is : Were they better for my life ?